Floss
Friends
The Shepherd Boy
One Summer Day
Emma's Lamb

These five favourite stories
are classic portrayals of
childhood on a farm.
Read about Floss, the
sheepdog; best friends Sam
and Alice, who find a newly
laid egg; James, who longs to
be a shepherd like his dad;
little Max and the big red
tractor; and Emma and
the lost lamb.

£14.99
UK ONLY

Days on the Farm

With thanks to the Manhattan Toy Company
who allowed their Floppy Bunny © to appear in *Friends*.

First published individually as *The Shepherd Boy* (1990), *Emma's Lamb* (1991),
Floss (1992), *One Summer Day* (1996) and *Friends* (1997) by Walker Books Ltd
87 Vauxhall Walk, London SE11 5HJ

This edition published 2001

2 4 6 8 10 9 7 5 3 1

© 1990, 1991, 1992, 1996, 1997, 2001 Kim Lewis

This book has been typeset in Sabon

Printed in Hong Kong

British Library Cataloguing in Publication Data:
a catalogue record for this book
is available from the British Library

ISBN 0-7445-8175-3

Days on the Farm

KIM LEWIS

WALKER BOOKS
AND SUBSIDIARIES
LONDON • BOSTON • SYDNEY

Contents

Floss

Page 11

Friends

Page 37

The Shepherd Boy

Page 63

One Summer Day

Page 89

Emma's Lamb

Page 115

Kim Lewis

Page 140

Floss

Floss was a young Border collie, who belonged to an old man in a town. She walked with the old man in the streets, and loved playing ball with children in the park.

14

"My son is a farmer,"
the old man told Floss.
"He has a sheepdog
who is too old to work.
He needs a young dog
to herd sheep on his farm.
He could train a
Border collie like you."

So Floss and the old man
travelled, away from
the town with
its streets and houses
and children playing ball
in the park.
They came to the
heather-covered hills
of a valley, where nothing
much grew except sheep.

Somewhere in her
memory, Floss knew
about sheep.
Old Nell soon showed
her how to round them up.
The farmer trained her
to run wide and lie down,
to walk on behind,
to shed, and to pen.
She worked very hard
to become a good sheepdog.

19

But sometimes Floss
woke up at night,
while Nell lay sound asleep.
She remembered
about playing with
children and rounding up
balls in the park.

22

The farmer took Floss
on the hill one day,
to see if she could gather
the sheep on her own.
She was rounding them
up when she heard a sound.
At the edge of the field
the farmer's children were
playing, with a brand new
black and white ball.

Floss remembered
all about children.
She ran to play with
their ball. She showed
off her best nose kicks,
her best passes. She
did her best springs
in the air.
"Hey, Dad, look at this!"
yelled the children.
"Look at Floss!"
The sheep started
drifting away.

The sheep escaped
through the gate and
into the yard. There
were sheep in the garden
and sheep on the road.
"FLOSS! LIE DOWN!"
The farmer's voice
was like thunder.
"You are meant for
work on this farm,
not play!"
He took Floss back to
the dog house.

28

Floss lay and worried
about balls and sheep.
She dreamt about
the streets of a town,
the hills of a valley,
children and farmers,
all mixed together,
while Nell had to round
up the straying sheep.

But Nell was too old
to work every day,
and Floss had to learn to
take her place.
She worked so hard
to gather sheep well,
she was much too tired
to dream any more.
The farmer was
pleased and ran Floss
in the dog trials.
"She's a good worker now,"
the old man said.

The children still wanted
to play with their ball.
"Hey, Dad," they asked,
"can Old Nell play now?"
But Nell didn't know
about children and play.
"No one can play ball
like Floss," they said.
"Go on, then," whispered
the farmer to Floss.
The children kicked the
ball high in the air.

Floss remembered
all about children.
She ran to play with
their ball.
She showed off her
best nose kicks,
her best passes.
She did her best
springs in the air.

Friends

Sam's friend Alice came to
play on the farm. They were in
the garden when they heard
loud clucking coming from
the hen house.

"Listen!" said Sam. "That means
a hen has laid an egg."

"An egg!" said Alice. "Let's
go and find it."

38

Sam and Alice
ran to the
hen house.

"Look," said Alice. "There's the egg!"

"I can put it in my hat," said Sam.

"I can put your hat in my bucket,"
  said Alice, "and put the bucket
  in the wheelbarrow."

"Then we can take it home,"
  said Sam.

The geese stood across the path.

"I'm afraid of geese," said Alice.

"Come on," said Sam. "We can go the long way round."

Alice pushed the wheel-
barrow through the trees.
"It's my turn now," said
Sam, and he pulled it
through the long grass
and thistles.

Together, they lifted it
over a ditch.

Sam and Alice went into the barn.

They were followed by Glen, the old farm dog.

"Is the egg all right?" asked Alice.

47

Sam and Alice
looked in the hat.
The egg was safe
and smooth,
without a crack.
"Look what we've found!"
said Alice, holding out
the egg to Glen.
"No!" cried Sam.
"He'll eat it!"

Sam reached out to take the egg.

Alice held it tight.

"It's mine!" said Sam.

"It's not!" said Alice. "I found it!"

"They're my hens!" said Sam,
pushing Alice.

SMASH went the egg as it fell on the ground. Glen started to eat it.

"I don't like you any more," said Alice. She picked up her bucket and went out of the barn.

Sam put on his empty hat. He did like Alice and he didn't like Alice and he felt he was going to cry.

Just then loud clucking
came from the hen house.
Sam ran out of the barn.
"Another egg!" he cried.
Sam and Alice looked at
each other.
"We can go and find it,"
said Sam.
"Yes, let's!" said Alice,
and smiled.

Sam put the egg
in his hat. He gave
the hat to Alice who
put it in her bucket.
They tiptoed past the geese and
Glen and walked back
to the house.

"What have you two been doing?" asked Mum.

"Finding eggs," said Sam.

"Together!" said Alice.

The Shepherd Boy

James' father was a shepherd. Every day he got up very early, took his crook and his collie, and went off to see his sheep.

James longed to be a shepherd too.

"You'll have to wait until you're a little older," his father said.

So every day James watched and waited.

James watched and waited all through spring. He watched as the new lambs were born, and saw them grow big and strong.

James watched and waited all through summer. He watched his father clip the sheep, and saw his mother pack the sacks of wool.

James watched and waited all through autumn. He watched his mother help to wean the lambs, and saw his father dip the sheep.

On market-day, James waited while the lambs were sold and heard the farmers talk of winter.

77

When snow fell, James watched his father feed the hungry sheep near the house, and saw him take hay on the tractor to the sheep on the hill.

Then James waited for his father to come home for tea.

On Christmas Day, James and his father and mother opened their presents under the tree.

James found a crook and a cap and a brand new dog-whistle of his very own.

In a basket in the barn,
James found a collie puppy.
James' father read the card
on the puppy's neck.

It said: *My name is Jess.*
I belong to a shepherd boy
called James.

When spring came
again, James got up very
early. He took his crook
and his cap, and called
Jess with his whistle.

85

Then James and his father went off to the fields together.

One Summer Day

90

One day Max saw a huge red tractor
with a plough roar by.
"Go out," said Max, racing to find
his shoes and coat and hat.
He hurried back to the window and looked out.

Two boys walked along with fishing-rods.

Max's friend Sara cycled past in the sun.

Max pressed his nose to the window,

but the tractor was gone.

As Max looked out, suddenly Sara looked in.

"Peekaboo!" she said.

Then Max heard a knock at the door.

"Can Max come out?"

"It's a summer day," laughed Sara,
helping Max take off his coat.
The sun was hot and
the grass smelled sweet.
Max and Sara walked down the farm road.

Max and Sara stopped to watch
the hens feeding.
One hen pecked at Max's foot.
"Shoo!" cried Max and sent the hens flapping.

Max and Sara ran through a field
where the grass was very high.
A cow with her calf mooed loudly.
Max made a small "Moo!" back.

Max and Sara
came to the river.
"Look, the boys
are fishing."
Sara caught Max
and took off his
shoes before he
ran in to paddle.

Then Max and Sara reached a gate.

Sara sat Max on top.

They heard a roar in the field

coming nearer and louder.

"Tractor!" shouted Sara and Max.

Max clung to the
gate as the tractor
loomed past.
It pulled a huge
plough which
flashed in the sun.
The field was
full of gulls.

"Let's go home," said Sara to Max.

They walked beside the freshly ploughed field,

along by the river and through the grass.

Sara carried Max back up the road.

"Tractor," sighed Max and closed his eyes.

Max woke up when they reached his house.

"Goodbye, Max," said Sara. "See you soon."

Max raced inside to the window.

Sara looked in as Max looked out.

"Peepo!" said Max, and pressed his nose to the glass.

113

Emma's Lamb

One rainy spring morning at lambing time,
Emma's father put a little lost lamb in a box
by the stove. Then he went back
to the field to look for Lamb's mother.

117

Lamb and Emma looked at each other.

"Baaa," said Lamb, sitting up in his box.

Emma wanted to keep little Lamb

and look after him all by herself.

119

So Emma dried Lamb
because he was very wet.
She tried to keep him warm
because he was very cold.
Emma fed Lamb
because he was very hungry.

121

When Lamb was dry and warm and fed,

he and Emma played.

"Baaa," said Lamb, getting

into a mess.

123

Then Emma took Lamb for a walk
and he skipped along behind her.
Emma decided to play hide and seek.
She closed her eyes and counted to ten.
"Here I come!" she cried.

Emma looked for Lamb in the stable.

She looked for him in the barn.

She looked for him in the granary.

She looked all around the yard.

127

She couldn't find Lamb in the house.

He wasn't in his box.

She couldn't find him in the
sheep pens either.

"I give up!" she shouted.

But Lamb was nowhere to be found.

Emma didn't want to play any more.

She wanted Lamb to come back.

She thought he might be cold and hungry.

"Where are you, Lamb?" she cried.

131

"Baaa," came a sound from the hayshed.

Emma ran inside to look.

Lamb sat up in the nesting box,

where the hens had laid their eggs.

"Baaa," he cried and ran to Emma.

134

"Lamb, I thought I'd lost you," said Emma,

holding him very tight.

She couldn't look after Lamb all by herself.

He needed to be with his mother.

But where was she?

Then Emma saw her father across the field.

A ewe without a lamb ran ahead of him, calling.

"Baaa," cried Lamb. He wriggled to get free.

Emma put him down,

and Lamb ran as fast as he could to his mother.

Emma went to the field the very next day.

When she called, Lamb came running to see her.

"Will you remember me?" asked Emma.

Lamb and Emma looked at each other.

"Baaa," said Lamb, waggling his tail.

Kim Lewis

I was born in Canada but now I live in a cottage on a beautiful hillside in
Northumberland with my husband and two children, our 700 sheep and 100 cows.

Because we live and work on a farm, the weather and the countryside are very much
a part of our lives and in my books I try to recreate the atmosphere and feeling
of living in a Northern landscape.

I write and draw about what I know and see around me, which is more amazing than
anything I could ever imagine in my head! I've always loved drawing animals,
but I also like to include those quiet corners of a farm which are not often seen in books –
the dark barns where tractors rest after work, where tools are stored and
where wool sacks are stacked.

Both my children are involved in farm life and it seemed very logical
that I should write about it in books for them. I also wanted other farm children
to recognize their own lives in the stories and for city children to be able to
"walk into" the books as if they were visiting a hill farm for themselves.

I hope you get as much pleasure from reading these stories
as I had in creating them.